Grow Up, David!

By David Shannon

THE BLUE SKY PRESS

An Imprint of Scholastic Inc. • New York

For my big brother, Mark, with love

AUTHOR'S NOTE

When I first started writing children's books, my mom sent me
a book I made when I was a little boy. It was illustrated with
drawings of "David" doing things I wasn't supposed to do. The
only words in it were "no" and "David" — those were the only
words I knew how to spell! That became the basis of the book
No, David! and led to several other books that celebrate
and explore the timeless, universal ways kids get in trouble.
Problems between siblings are the stuff of legends,
or — in David's case — typical family life. David can't do
everything his big brother can. On the other hand, he can
get away with things his older sibling can't. Rules change,
but one thing stays the same — no matter how much
David grows up, he'll always be the "little" brother.

THE BLUE SKY PRESS

Celebrating 25 Years of Award-winning Publishing

Library of Congress catalog card number: 2017042052
ISBN 978-1-338-25097-8
10 9 8 7 6 5 4 3 2 1   18 19 20 21 22
Printed in China   62
First edition, September 2018

big
David's brother
            ^
always said . . .

No, David!

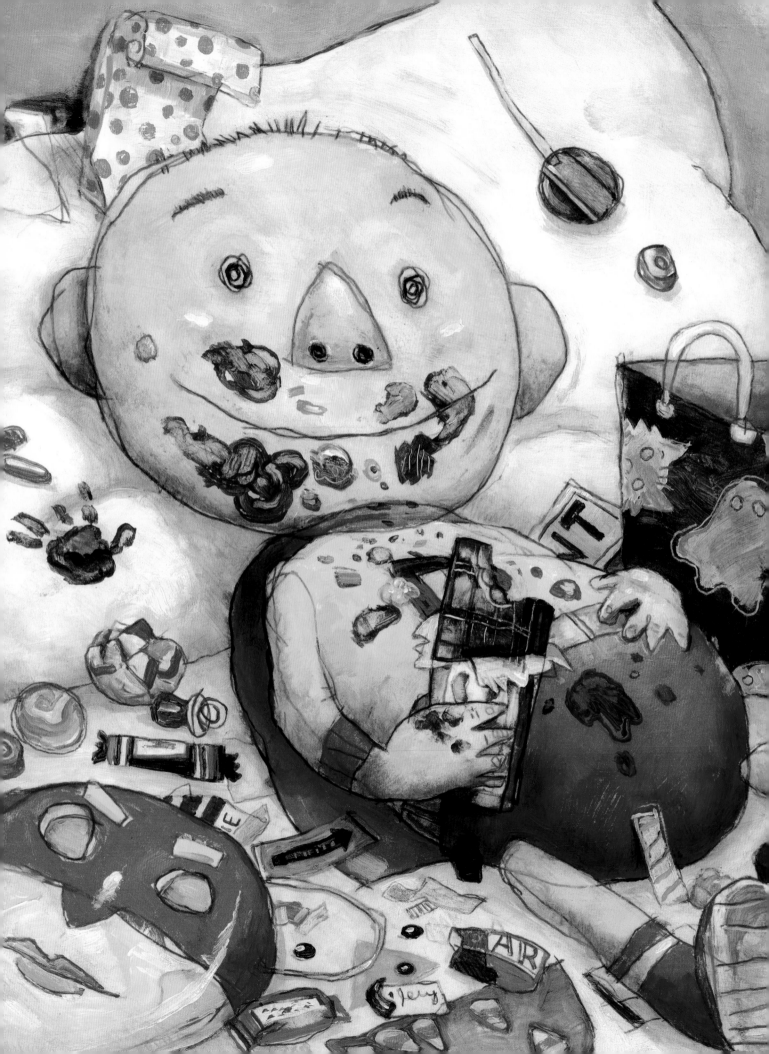

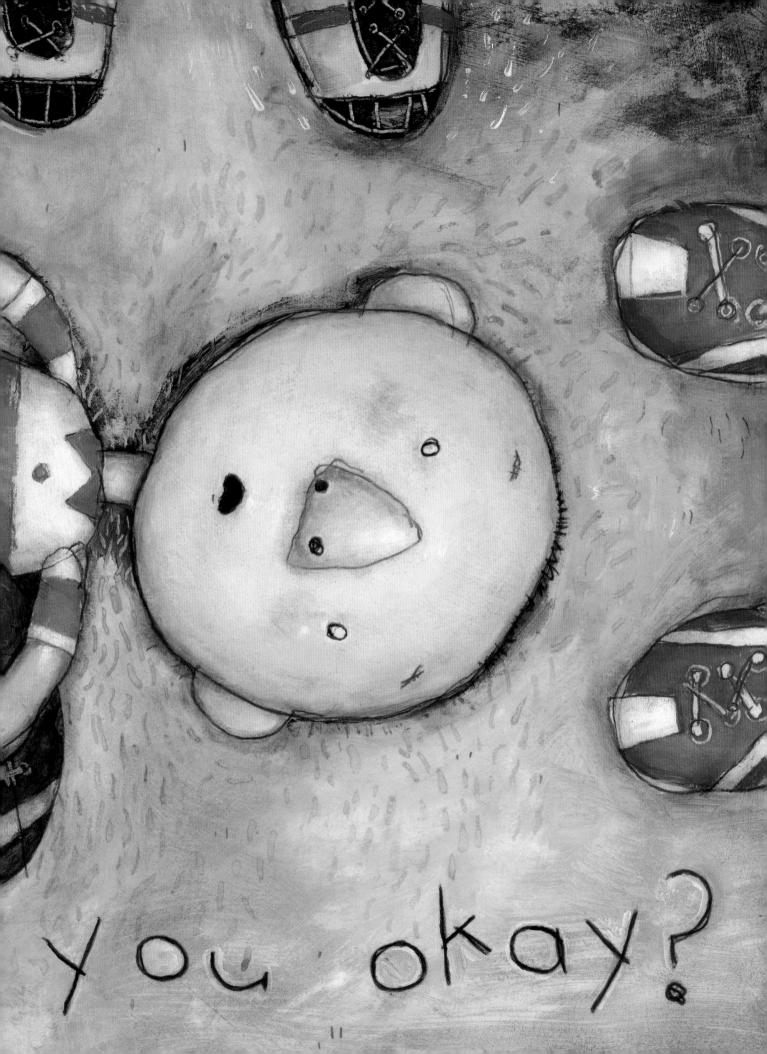